GReeDY ZeBRa

HODDER CHILDREN'S BOOKS

First published in Great Britain in 1984 by Hodder Children's Books
This edition published in 2017 by Hodder and Stoughton

38

Text copyright © Bruce Hobson, 1984
Illustrations copyright © Adrienne Kennaway, 1984

A CIP catalogue record for this book
is available from the British Library.

ISBN 978 0 340 40912 1

Printed in China

MIX
Paper from
responsible sources
FSC® C104740
FSC
www.fsc.org

Hodder Children's Books
An imprint of
Hachette Children's Group
Part of Hodder and Stoughton
Carmelite House
50 Victoria Embankment
London EC4Y 0DZ

An Hachette UK Company
www.hachette.co.uk

www.hachettechildrens.co.uk

GREEDY ZEBRA

By
Mwenye Hadithi

Illustrated by
Adrienne Kennaway

*Hodder
Children's
Books*

Long, long ago, all the animals in the world
were a dull, depressing colour; no coats, no horns,
no spots and no stripes. Just dull and dusty. Until. . .

One stormy day in the heart of the leafy forests of Africa there was a great rumbling in the earth, and all of a sudden a huge cave appeared in the ground.

A few of the animals crept cautiously up to this new and wonderful sight, and when the bravest of them peered into the darkness he saw something glittering amongst the rocks.

The cave was full of furs
and skins, all glossy and new!
Stepping inside, he came across
horns and tails of countless
shapes and sizes, and needles and
threads of a thousand different colours.
Trembling with excitement, he rushed
out to tell the other animals
what he had seen.

The news spread far and wide, and soon all
the animals were on their way to see the cave,
running and jumping and sliding and swinging,
and slithering through the trees.

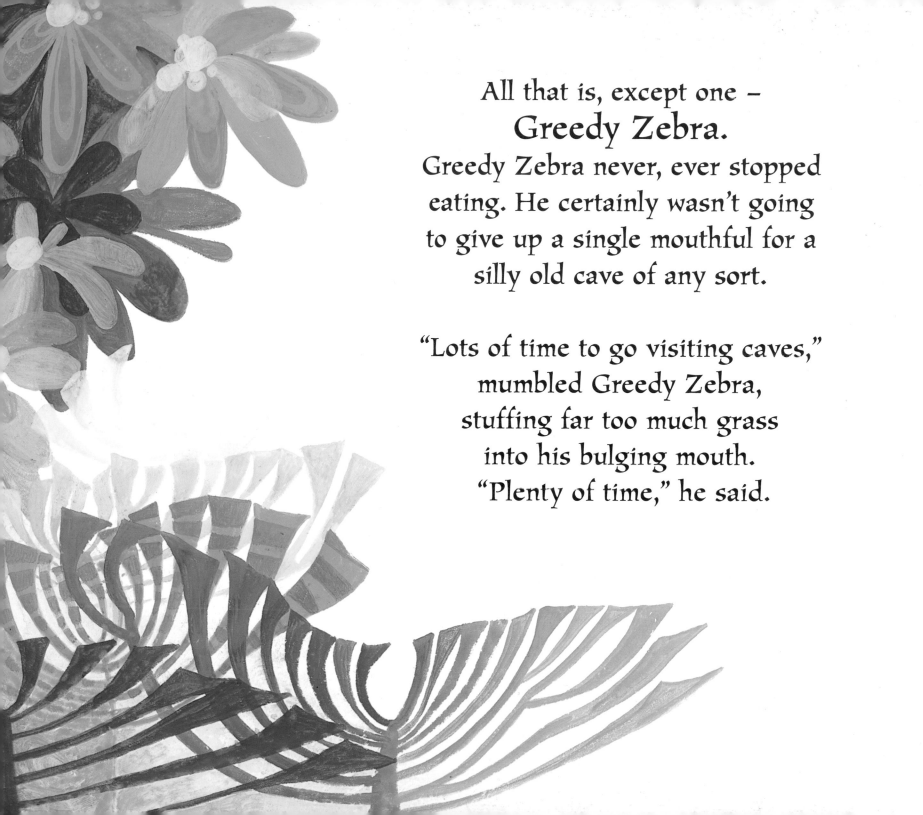

All that is, except one –
Greedy Zebra.
Greedy Zebra never, ever stopped
eating. He certainly wasn't going
to give up a single mouthful for a
silly old cave of any sort.

"Lots of time to go visiting caves,"
mumbled Greedy Zebra,
stuffing far too much grass
into his bulging mouth.
"Plenty of time," he said.

Soon all the animals in the jungle were gathered at the mouth of the cave, waiting for Elephant to speak. Elephant was the one who knew everything because Eagle told him all the secrets of the Spirit of the Mists. He coughed pompously, and addressed the gathering. "It is time for you all to have coats," he said. "There are all kinds of materials here from which you may choose. You will be issued with needles by Rabbit, but there is only one needle each, so take good care of it. Now you may go in – but no shoving and pushing, and keep in an orderly line!"

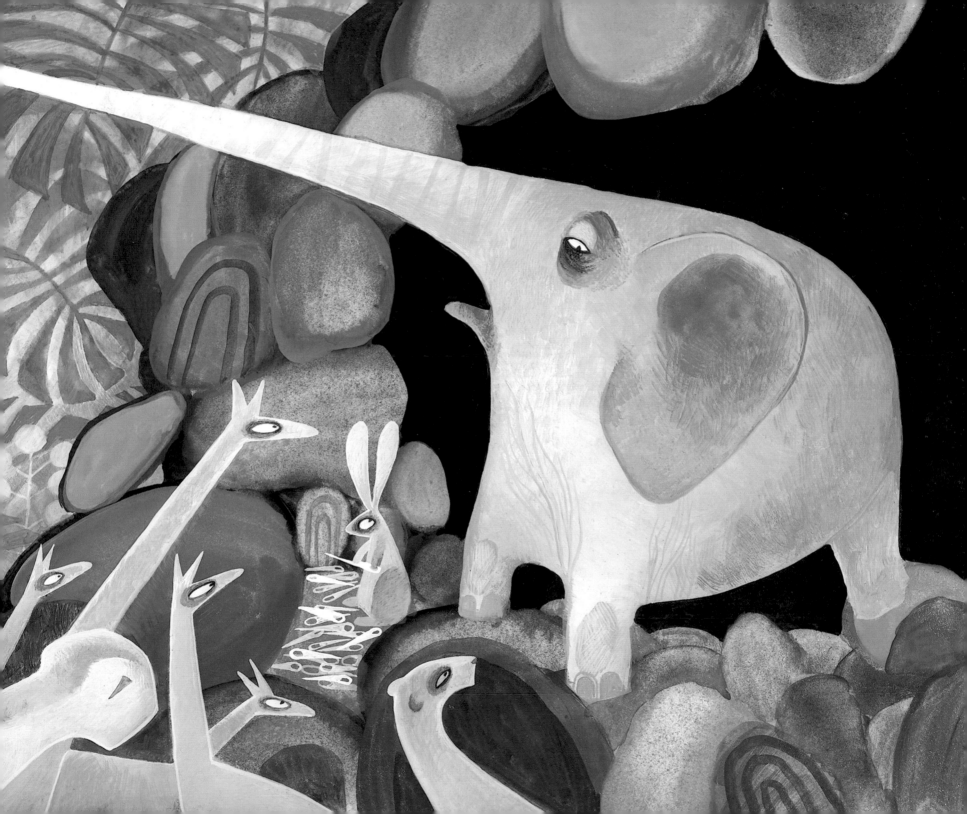

Meanwhile, Greedy Zebra was still eating.
"Munch, munch," he went. "This
particular grass is so delicious. . . "
He stopped to gape at the beautiful thing
in front of him. It couldn't be! But it was
Sable the antelope, and she was wearing
the most glorious new coat. And horns!
She was wearing horns!

When Greedy Zebra heard that the coat and
the horns came from the cave, he trotted off
as fast as his fat little legs
could carry him.

But he couldn't
resist a leaf here,
or a succulent
blade of
grass there.
Oh and that
patch was
too good to
pass by without
one little bite!

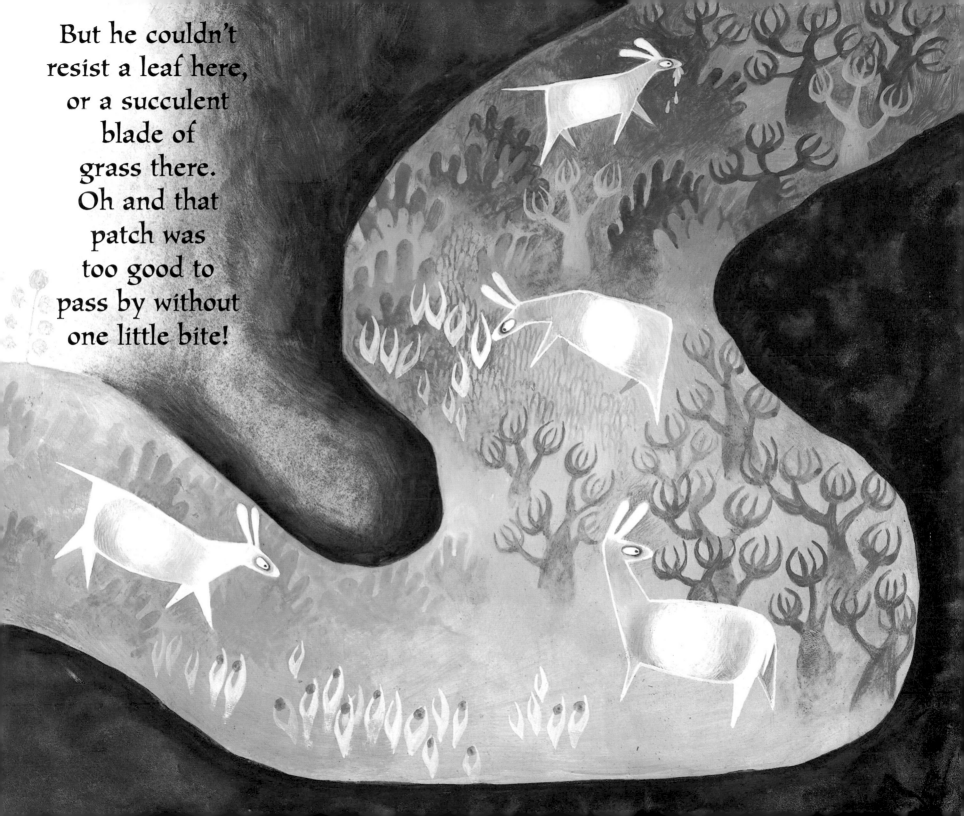

From time to time he met another, and another. . .

and
yet
another. . .

. . .of the wonderfully clothed animals. Stopping for a last
bite not far from the cave, he watched Leopard finish her sewing.
Leopard, as careful as usual, had sewn the most splendid fur coat
with spots all over it. Greedy Zebra could hardly believe his eyes as
he watched Leopard wriggle into the perfectly fitting fur.

"I shall have spots like that," he said to himself,
and he hurried off, eager to reach the cave.

"Delicious," he munched, smacking his chubby lips.

But it was a hot day, so he stopped for a cool drink at a stream and there he came across a patch of the greenest grass he had ever seen.

Back at the cave most of the animals were leaving.

Only Rhino and Elephant were
still cutting their material. They had
chosen a very strong grey cloth. Poor old Rhino, who was very
short-sighted, had stuck his horns on any old how and was having a
terrible time. He was too nervous to ask Elephant for help, because he
knew that the pompous animal would only make fun of him. He had dropped
his needle and the more frantically he searched, the further into the bushes
he kicked it. He put on the baggy coat, and shuffled off in a very bad mood.

Just then Greedy Zebra trotted by,
with blades of grass bulging from his mouth.

"I'll have spots like Leopard," he was saying.
"And horns like Kudu, a mane like Lion and a tail like
Cheetah. I shall be the finest looking animal in the forest!"

And at the risk of indigestion he gave a short gallop into the cave.

Then he stopped, aghast.

There was nothing left!
No horns, no fine cloth
– nothing. Frantically he
searched through the cave, but all he could
find were a few strips of black material. Forlornly he cut
them all to the same size and stitched them together.

"It looks very tight," he thought nervously to himself. Being such a very fat zebra, he had a terrible time squeezing into his coat. He pushed and grunted and oohed and aahed and – POP, he was inside it. But what a tight fit! It was nearly bursting at the seams around his fat tummy. He trotted down to the stream to take a quick bite of a leafy bush – and POP, his coat burst open.

His tubby tummy
squeezed through
the seams. How the monkeys roared
with laughter!

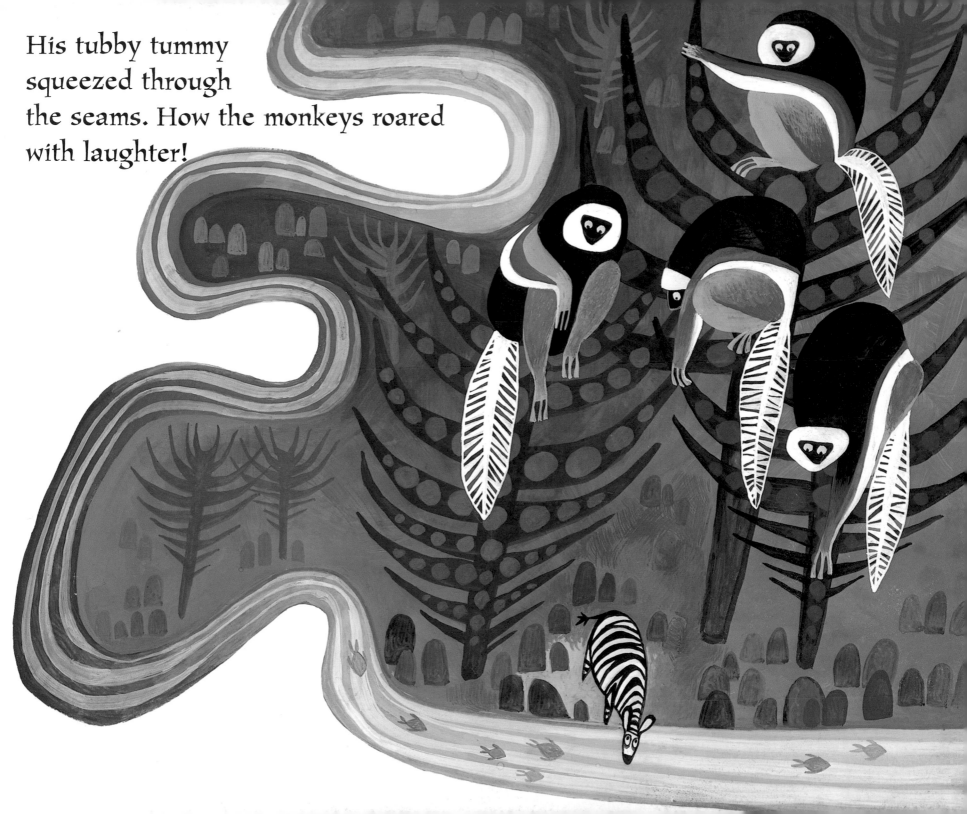

To this day his chubby stomach shines through his coat because he is so greedy.